Terrible Tiger

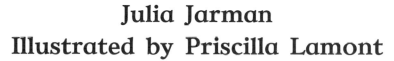

Julia Jarman
Illustrated by Priscilla Lamont

RIGBY

There is a terrible tiger under my bed.

I can see his tail.

I can see his head.

"Terrible Tiger, go away!

Terrible Tiger, please don't stay!"

I can see his teeth in his terrible jaws.

I can see his feet with their terrible claws.

"Terrible Tiger, go away!
Terrible Tiger, please don't stay!"

Then I see him **S-T-R-E-T-C-H** his jaws.

Then I see him **S-T-R-E-T-C-H** his claws.

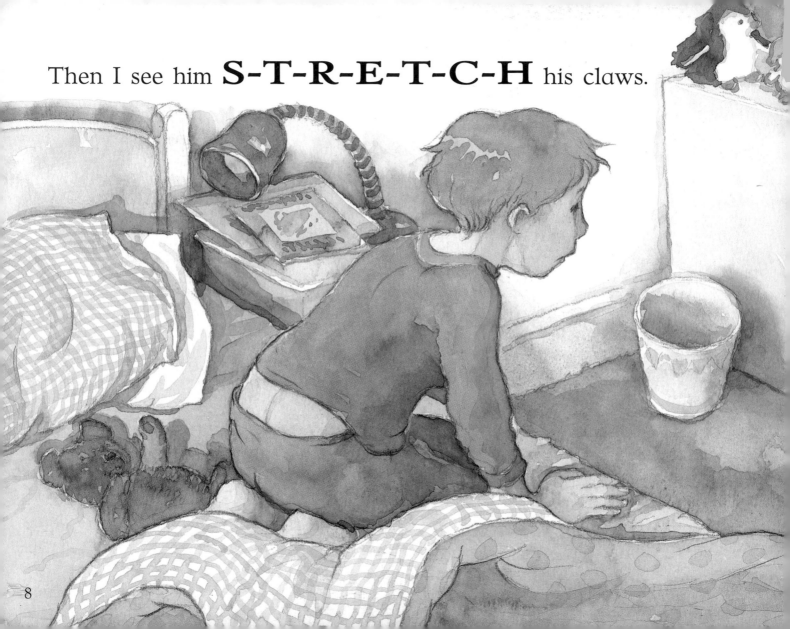

I see him shake his terrible head.
What is he doing under my bed?

The tiger says, "I want to go.
But I am stuck.
The bed is too low."

I pull the tiger.

I get him out.

Then I hear my mother shout.

"It's time to sleep," my mother said.

Now there is no tiger under the bed.

The tiger is under my covers instead.